The Wisdom of Mulla Nasruddin

Shahrukh Husain

Illustrations Shilpa Ranade

SCHOLASTIC
New York Toronto London Auckland Sydney
Mexico City New Delhi Hong Kong Buenos Aires

Text © 2006 Shahrukh Husain
Illustrations © 2006 Scholastic India Pvt. Ltd.

All rights reserved.

Published by Scholastic India Pvt. Ltd.
A subsidiary of Scholastic Inc., New York, 10012 (USA).
Publishers since 1920, with international operations in Canada, Australia, New Zealand, the United Kingdom, Mexico, India, Argentina and Hong Kong.

No part of this publication may be reproduced in whole or in part, or stored in a retrieval system, or transmitted in any form or by any means, electronic, mechanical, photocopying, recording, or otherwise without the written permission of the publisher.

For information regarding permission, write to:
Scholastic India Pvt. Ltd.
Golf View Corporate Tower-A, 3rd Floor,
DLF Phase-V, Gurgaon 122002 (India)

Typeset by Mantra Virtual Services Pvt Ltd

First edition: September 2006
Reprint: December 2006

ISBN: 81-7655-570-3
Rs 100

Printed at, Dot Scan. New Dehli

Contents

Introduction v

The Heat of a Candle 1
Don't Do as I Say 9
Earthly Glory 12
Mind Who Sees You 15
What Is Equal? 17
Who's the Fool? 20
The Uses of Wisdom 26
The Honourable Coat 31
Up and Down 35
Upholding the Law 39
The Greater Need 43
Where There Is Light 46

Tricking the Mulla	48
The Fruit of the Tree	51
The End of the World	55
Let the Turban Speak	59
Strange Town, Strange Ways	61
Fair Exchange	64
The Eternal Duck	70
The Runaway Basket	77
New Clothes	81
Dying to Keep	84
The Life of a Pot	88
The Rules of the Game	91
The Donkey's Load	94

Introduction

The mention of Mulla Nasruddin is often met with a smile. There are thousands of stories about the Mulla, retold by hundreds of people the world over. What makes them unique is that hidden inside the wit and the tomfoolery is true wisdom, if we take the trouble to look for it.

Who is this much-loved figure? Where does he come from? Is he a historical figure or is he fictional?

There are very few facts. The Arabs, Afghans, Greeks, Iranians and Turks all claim he is theirs. They all call him by local titles but mostly he is Mulla Nasruddin or Nasruddin Hoja—both titles mean 'teacher' or 'preacher'. He is believed to be a Sufi, who lived between 1208-1284 and wandered the world. He had a great passion for truth and his simplicity was so extreme that he often appeared foolish.

Most people think he comes from Turkey, from Sivrihisar where the inhabitants are known to be a little strange, or from Eshkishehir. The first written mention of him is said to appear in a manuscript dated 1480, called the *Saltukname*.

The facts don't really matter. Like all true folk heroes, he belongs to all of us. Stories about him have been passed around orally for seven hundred years. Like all stories that spread by word of mouth, they continually change to suit the moment, or the teller's purpose. The character changes, too, acquiring the qualities of specific societies. For example, a wife or a parent may be added, another one removed. So we see the Mulla young and old; he is patient, brave, helpful or grumpy, mocking and greedy. His stories are like a mirror, reflecting the problems of society- poverty, snobbery, narrow-mindedness and ignorance.

Whichever way you approach the Mulla's tales, they are sure to be enriching. And be sure to pass on your favourite ones to someone else.

✲✶❯ The Heat of a Candle ❮✶✲

Mulla Nasruddin gazed out on the icy crags through the window of the coffeehouse.

'Look,' he said to the gathered townspeople, watching the sunset. 'How beautiful it is out there! The sun looks like a glowing ball of fire. See how it touches the sky with a pink glow.'

The gathered men grunted. 'You are mad, Nasruddin,' Ali said, who lived across the square from him. 'There's nothing beautiful about it. The weather is ice cold, the crops will frost over and we'll all die of hunger if we don't freeze to death first.'

The others nodded, as they huddled as close to the fire as possible. One of them prodded it with a poker so that the flames leaped higher and higher.

'Nonsense!' exclaimed Nasruddin. 'We're all healthy men. As long as we dress properly and keep our bodies moving, we can come to no harm.'

'Are you saying you don't feel the cold like the rest of us?' Davut challenged.

The Mulla smiled, spreading his palms to draw their gaze to himself. 'Look at me, my friends. I'm not as fit as some of you, nor as well clothed. But am I trying to climb into the fire like you? Have you seen me even once, prodding the flames, or holding my coffee cup to my cheeks to warm my face? I don't think so.'

'That's all very well, Mulla,' said Emir, Nasruddin's next-door neighbour who was tall and thin. 'But aren't you worried about food? Our rations are not going to last all winter, yet we need decent food to fuel our bodies if we are to survive this terrible weather.'

The Mulla laughed out loud. 'Fuel, food, what are you talking about? You're a young, fit man. Look at the size of you. Get out into the woods; chop down a few trees for firewood. I promise you, carrying it back up the hill to your house will be enough to warm you up for many hours. What is all this gloom about? As for me, I welcome the winter. It is a time for me to make myself fit and to test the spirit.'

'Are you saying you don't feel the cold, like the rest of us?' Davut repeated.

'That would seem to be what I am saying,' replied Nasruddin. 'The cold weather is not a trial for me as it is for the rest of you.'

'I think the Mulla is merely boasting,' croaked an old man, Etki, who would have fallen into the fire if he'd moved an inch closer.

'Say what you like,' Nasruddin insisted. 'I feel what I feel; you feel what you feel. It's the way God made us.'

'But,' said Etki, shuffling his bottom around so that he could face Nasruddin, 'you could prove to all of us for once and all, that you are not merely boasting.'

All eyes turned to the old man.

'Tell me how,' the Mulla asked, interestedly, 'and it shall be done.'

'Well,' said Etki, 'you could stand outside in the square when night falls. But you shall be there without fire or flame to warm you until the sun's rays announce dawn. And if you succeed in doing that, the entire town will contribute something to you from their winter rations so that you will have a more luxurious winter than you have ever had before. If you fail, then you will have to treat the whole town to a fabulous meal.' He looked round at the others. 'Is that agreed?'

A murmur of agreement went round the room.

Nasruddin could see that no one believed he would succeed in the task. 'I agree,' he replied. 'When would you like to put me to the test?'

'Wait a moment, Mulla,' Etki said. 'Listen to the conditions first. You will stay out alone, from dusk till dawn. You will not have any extra coats or blankets. Your wife will not be allowed to bring you food or tea or anything to warm you.'

'I agree,' said Nasruddin. 'Just me, the clothes I wear everyday including this patchy coat and the old blanket I carry around my shoulders, and God's protection.'

'We all know you have a way with words,' said Davut. 'So we will watch from our windows all night just to make sure there is no trickery.'

Nasruddin agreed. 'No trickery.'

It was almost dusk, so they all trooped out of the coffeehouse and into the town square where Nasruddin took up his position. The others hurried into their homes and shut the doors and windows tight against the cold.

Alone, with only the moon for company and a

dozen pair of eyes watching him from their warm rooms, Nasruddin jumped up and down, threw his arms about and ran in circles round the square, to keep the blood circulating in his veins.

Nasruddin was no newcomer to discomfort. In his time, he had travelled steep mountains encased in rocks and sheets of ice. He had slept beneath glaciers as cold mountain winds screamed and howled like wild monsters, buffeting him as hard and as violently as a wrestler in a ring, so that he rocked from side to side, and was in danger of falling off the precipice. He was hardly going to be daunted by this tame little town square surrounded by houses which acted as windbreaks. And if in return he was to be rewarded with enough food to last all winter, then why should he complain?

So he kept up his running and jumping, throwing in the odd somersault and cartwheel to break the monotony. He also touched his toes, did push-ups and sit-ups. And then the first rays of sunlight broke the dark pall of night and everything became visible again.

Mulla Nasruddin walked into the coffeehouse and waited for the townspeople to arrive.

'Are you convinced now?' he demanded as they trooped in. 'That I can truly withstand the cold?'

'Convinced of what?' jeered Davut. 'That you'd

make a good clown?'

Nasruddin was angered at his rudeness. He replied quietly. 'Did I prove to you that I could survive a night out in the cold without fire or food to warm me?'

'You did not,' replied Davut. The rest of the group yelled out their agreement.

Nasruddin rubbed his beard. 'Okay,' he said. 'Tell me where I failed. Did I not stay out all night?'

'That you did,' Davut said.

'Did I have any extra clothes for warmth?'

'You did not.'

'Did my wife bring me food or fire?'

'She did not.'

'So where would you say I failed the test?'

Etki thrust his way through the crowd. 'We watched as you ran about, Nasruddin. At first we thought it was just another one of your strange little ways to amuse yourself and stay warm.'

Nasruddin nodded.

'But soon we noticed that you always stopped a little longer near a flame in a window by the square,' the old man said, slyly. 'And that is where you stopped to perform most of your antics. You were warming yourself at the fire.'

Nasruddin looked puzzled. 'But the house nearest the square must be at less five hundred feet away!

And the flame was a tiny flickering candle that barely cast enough light to illuminate the windowpane!'

'You see!' shouted Davut triumphantly. 'You know exactly which house and which light I'm talking about! You have been caught out in your trick.'

Nasruddin looked round the room. 'Is that what you all think?' he asked.

'We do,' they agreed.

Nasruddin smiled graciously. 'Then you must be right,' he said. 'I will accept your verdict. I will be delighted to welcome you all to dinner at my house tonight.'

That night everyone turned up at Nasruddin's house, pleased with the way they had handled the whole business. The Mulla was famous for his excellent cooking and his generous table, and everyone expected a fabulous meal. Ayshe, Nasruddin's wife, was enraged at her husband for inviting the men who had treated him so badly, and so was lurking in the back room, tidying furiously.

The guests and the host were all in high spirits and they laughed and joked through the first hour and the second. By the time three hours had gone by, the guests started falling silent through sheer hunger, though the same reason made their stomachs rumble loudly. Everyone, except the Mulla, gradually became grumpy because it was way past their dinnertime.

Finally, Etki could bear it no longer and sneaked into the kitchen to see how dinner was coming along. An enormous cauldron hung over the fire, filled to the brim with wonderful ingredients.

The old man's stomach rumbled loudly at the sight. He turned to see Nasruddin at the kitchen door.

'What's the delay, Mulla?' he asked. 'Your guests have been waiting three hours.'

'I know,' replied Nasruddin. 'It's still cooking.'

Etki looked closely at the pot. There was no steam coming from it, and neither was the liquid bubbling. He leaned forward and touched the pot and leapt up in shock.

'This hasn't even begun to warm up!' he yelled.

The Mulla nodded, sagely. 'But we must be patient.'

The old man began to splutter. He bent down creakily to check the cooking fire.

There was only a lone candle flickering under the pot.

'How do you expect to cook such a huge pot of food with this tiny candle?' asked Etki angrily.

'The same way, my friend, that you expected it to warm me from behind a windowpane five hundred feet away,' replied the Mulla.

Don't Do As I Say

Mulla Nasruddin was famous for being a bit odd. You could say that his mind worked very differently from that of other people. This was the most likely reason that he behaved in a way that people often found strange and hard to understand. Some put it down to the fact that he came from Sivrihisar. Everyone knew the people of that region were very strange indeed; they dressed strangely and they talked strangely and their entire conduct was bizarre. But most wise men agreed that beneath the apparent foolishness of Mulla Nasruddin was clarity of insight that cut straight to the heart of the truth. Sometimes though, one had to ponder before one understood the inner wisdom of his remarks and ways.

When Nasruddin was a boy, he helped his father carry merchandise back and forth from the cities where the goods were made to those where they were sold. Even then, Nasruddin did exactly as he wanted and not as he was told to. If he did not agree with what he was commanded to do, he would do things his own way—even if it was his father's orders he was disobeying.

'What is wrong with the boy?' spluttered Nasruddin's father in exasperation to his wife and friends. 'He does exactly the opposite of what I say.'

'Then the best thing is to reverse your commands,' everyone advised. 'Tell him you want him to go right if you wish him to go left and command him to stand still when you want him to walk on.'

So that is what the old merchant did.

On the whole, this method worked reasonably well. Nasruddin galloped along at a great speed when his father asked him to slow down, and loaded the goods on to the donkeys when he was told to leave them in the store, and remained very quiet when his father invited him to converse. And so the partnership became very workable though the old man wished that he did not have to work in such a contrary way just to get the simplest things done smoothly.

One day, as Nasruddin and his father were driving their donkeys across a fast-moving stream, the pannier on the back of one of the donkeys began to slip.

'Nasruddin!' yelled the old merchant, thinking hard to frame his command so that it was the opposite of what he wanted done. 'Quick! The bags of flour are slipping into the water. Press down on them!'

Immediately, Nasruddin reached out and pressed hard on the pannier carrying the flour. The fastening unloosened with his weight, and the bags of flour came away and fell into the river.

'Heavens, boy!' yelled Nasruddin's father. 'Why, in the name of Almighty God, did you do that?'

Nasruddin looked directly into his father's face. 'Because, Father, I thought you should realise how foolish your orders are.'

Earthly Glory

Mulla Nasruddin's fortunes changed all the time. Days of wealth were followed by seasons of poverty. Weeks of comfortable family life in a decent house dissolved into years of travel where he had nowhere to lay his head and only the charity of strangers to rely upon. He could play host to his entire town during one period and at other times, he had to stand in a marketplace with hands extended for a few coins. Good times, bad times, they were sent by God to take care of the more important qualities of humankind, to purge pride and heighten humility. Indeed, God moved in strange ways.

And here was Nasruddin, in a strange coffeehouse, in a strange town. He had found a few coins in his pocket, earned from giving someone a ride on his donkey, and he was looking forward to his meal.

The coffeehouse was somewhat rundown but he had noticed they offered rice steamed with a blend of herbs, spices and beans on their menu. Not that he needed to look at the menu, the exquisite aroma was irresistible to a man who had lived off little more than scraps for the last few days. No matter that it was only rice with beans and not meat or chicken!

He settled into his chair, eating some freshly baked bread and looking around him while he waited for his meal. His gaze fell on a grandly dressed man swaggering about in the street, trying to impress the people in the market square.

Nasruddin noticed interestedly that the man's trousers were so baggy that they must have used up half a bolt of brocade. And the rest of the bolt, no doubt, had been used for his shirt and turban. As for his jacket, it glittered and glowed as if it had come from the Pasha himself.

Nasruddin must have spoken out loud, because the man who put his steaming platter of rice on the table before him replied, 'It does indeed come from the Pasha. He is the sultan's footman.'

The man was sitting down now, at the plush inn across the road. He had demanded a large table to be set just for him. A massive platter of rice was placed before him, surrounded with spit-roasted chicken and lamb and aubergines and courgettes and succulent bell-peppers.

Nasruddin looked down at his own plate of rice, studded here and there with beans. It seemed to have shrunk somewhat. He lifted the first morsel to his mouth with the word *'b'ismillah!'* on his lips. In the name of God.

'Indeed, God,' he said. 'You are merciful and beneficent and I am grateful for your kindness. But it is true you move in mysterious ways. You are the greatest and most powerful and generous. Yet, look at the difference between the sultan's servant there— and your own humble servant here.'

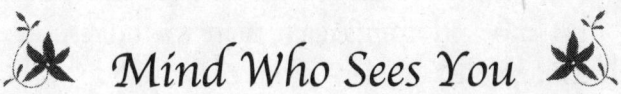 Mind Who Sees You

One day, on his long wanderings, Mulla Nasruddin was far from home. The sun was high in the sky, and he was hot and hungry. He saw some houses in the distance and decided he would stop at one of them and ask for shelter. Since it was the custom of Muslims to feed and shelter travellers in the name of God, he imagined a cool bowl of yoghurt, a refreshing wash and a place to lay down his head, and thought this would make his journey seem shorter.

Sure enough, the uphill climb seemed to be less toilsome than he expected. The Mulla finally stopped and looked at the houses around him. 'Which one?' he asked himself, as his gaze swept the dwellings and came to rest on a mansion.

'That's the one,' he decided. 'The owners of that house will have no trouble sparing me something.'

Suddenly, it was as if his feet had wings. He practically flew to the door of the mansion. Then he knocked and waited.

Several minutes passed. There was no response.

He knocked again. Again, there was no response. He thought he saw a face at one of the windows, but no one came to open the door.

Nasruddin called out. 'Hello, in there. There's a tired traveller at your door, in need of shelter and a bite to eat.'

The door opened and a servant appeared. 'I'm afraid I can't help,' he said. 'My master is away on business.'

'Your master is out?' asked Nasruddin.

'That's what I said, isn't it?' snapped the servant.

'In that case,' Nasruddin replied, 'here's some free advice. Tell your master from Mulla Nasruddin, next time he goes away, he should take his face with him. If he leaves it at the window like this time, someone will surely steal it.'

What Is Equal

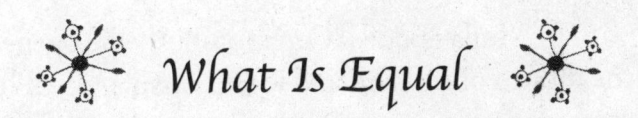

Four small boys came up to Mulla Nasruddin one morning. They were dragging an enormous sack of walnuts between them.

'Will you please help us?' they begged.

'Well that depends on what you want me to do,' said the Mulla.

'You see this bag of nuts?' they said. 'They're for all of us to share. But we don't know how to distribute them between the four of us.'

'It will be my pleasure,' agreed Mulla Nasruddin.

'But first I have a question to ask.'

'Anything Mulla,' Mehmet, one of the boys, said.

'Well now,' began the Mulla, 'let's get it all clear. You want me to distribute these nuts amongst you? Is that right?'

The boys nodded, eagerly.

'I can do that. But first you must tell me—do you want me to share them out in God's way or the way of humankind?'

'God's way!' the boys chorused, without exception.

The Mulla nodded. Ceremoniously, he opened the mouth of the sack and looked inside. Then he reached in and gave a fistful of walnuts to Yusuf. Then another.

'Thank you, Mulla, thank you!' the boy said, delighted, scrabbling around to pick up the walnuts that had rolled out of his hands.

The Mulla was already reaching into the sack again. He held out his fist to Mehmet, who reached out with open palms. The Mulla emptied his fist and there, in the centre of the boy's palm were about three walnuts. Mehmet was disappointed. Maybe the Mulla would make up for it with the second handful. In went the Mulla's hand. And here it came. But no!

The Mulla was holding out his hand to Isa, the third boy, whose palms were filled to overflowing.

'Hold up your shirt,' the Mulla told Eli, as the others looked on in surprise.

The Mulla picked up the sack and tipped the remaining walnuts into his shirt.

'There you are!' he said, beaming all over his face. 'A job done well.' And off he went.

The boys ran after him. 'Mulla! Mulla! Please wait!'

'I thought it was just one favour you wanted,' the Mulla said, somewhat grumpily. 'I do have my own work to attend to, you know.'

'But Mulla,' Mehmet said. 'We wanted the nuts to be shared out fairly. That's why we asked you to do the job.'

'Ah,' said the Mulla. 'Then you should have asked me to distribute them in the way of humankind.'

Who's the Fool?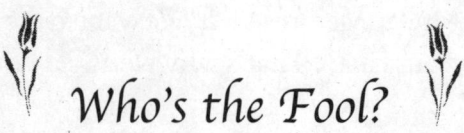

Mulla Nasruddin was walking past the mosque one day when he saw a large crowd. Above the silence of the crowd, he could hear a loud voice admonishing '... then beat them!'

'Beat who?' the Mulla asked Davut, one of the townspeople whom he recognised at the edge of the crowd.

'Your child,' the man muttered. 'That is Mulla Halil, and he is a famous speaker.'

'What nonsense,' the Mulla thought. 'Why should

I beat my child?'

The Mulla could see how the man was straining to listen to the speaker and didn't want to engage in a debate with him. So he edged into the centre of the crowd, to listen.

Mulla Halil was a tall man with an even taller hat. He was flailing his arms around, so that the people standing near him had to jump back to avoid being smacked.

'If your children lie to you,' Halil thundered, 'I say, don't stop to consider how best to deal with this. The only way to teach them a lesson they will remember for the rest of their lives, is to give them a good beating.'

The Mulla looked at the intent faces around him, listening to the speaker rant. The old man Etki was shaking his head in agreement. Emir, his tall neighbour, was listening with his mouth open.

Nasruddin couldn't bear to let this man give his fellow townsmen such bad advice. 'People believe men who put themselves up on a pedestal and start preaching as if they are the ultimate authority,' he thought. 'I cannot stay quiet or all the children here will soon be walking around covered in blue and yellow bruises.'

The Mulla raised his voice. 'Excuse me, sir, but how can you tell for sure that a child is lying?'

The speaker was shocked by the interruption. He screwed up his eyes and stared into the crowd to see who had spoken. Etki helpfully pointed to the Mulla with his walking stick, so he soon spotted the Mulla in his odd clothes.

Halil laughed rudely. 'If you do not know the difference between a lie and the truth, how do you dare to call yourself a Mulla?'

'Well, sir,' replied the Mulla. 'If you were to tell me that you are an educated man from Istanbul and that you were born in Konya, how would I know if you lie or tell the truth? For a man may be born in Konya but if he grows up in Istanbul, he speaks like a native of the city. So, must I be beaten if I tell my neighbour that today I met a man from Istanbul? What I mean is, a child, or an adult for that matter, may believe he is telling the truth but what he believes to be true may, for many reasons, be an honest mistake.'

'You talk nonsense,' Halil shouted. 'The good people here know what I'm talking about.'

'And there's something else,' the Mulla continued, as if he hadn't heard a word of what the man said. 'I don't hold with beating anyone, least of all children. There are other ways of teaching children a lesson.'

'Look, old man,' the speaker said. 'If you had the answers, you would be standing up here talking to the people, not I.'

Etki and Davut cackled in agreement.

'Precisely,' said the Mulla, who was famous for trying to avoid making speeches. 'So I won't say another word.' But he was happy to have planted doubt in the minds of the people and content, he turned to go.

'Oi there!' shouted Halil. 'Too afraid to lose the argument, are you?'

The Mulla turned around sharply. 'Not at all,' he replied. 'But this is your soapbox, not mine. I am quite happy to continue this discussion. Why don't you come to my humble home tomorrow and there we can argue to our heart's content over a meal.'

The next day, Halil arrived at Mulla Nasruddin's house, along with two or three of his cronies, and banged on the door.

'Ho! Mulla, get your arguments sharpened. I'm here.' He stood back and waited for the door to open, while his friends grinned and raised their eyebrows. But the door remained firmly shut.

Halil banged again, harder. Again, there was no answer.

His friends looked in through the windows, cupping their palms on top of their eyes to see better through the glass.

'There's no one here,' said one. 'He could have

gone to the market to buy food for our feast.'

Another friend disagreed. 'The Mulla's pulled a fast one! He's disappeared.'

Halil kicked and banged at the door. 'Come out at once, Mulla!' he shouted.

The house remained silent. The Mulla was not there.

Finally, Mulla Halil gave up. 'I will pay him back for his ill manners,' he swore. 'He will be the laughing stock of the town. He will not be able to show his ugly little face anywhere.'

He pulled a piece of charcoal from his pocket. In large, bold letters, he wrote his message on the door for all to see. Then he stepped back and roared with laughter.

'FOOL,' read the message.

'To the market, lads,' Halil said triumphantly. 'Our work is not yet done. Let us spread the news of the Mulla's shame.'

And off they went, laughing loudly and repeating their experience to everyone who would listen.

Halil and his friends went to look for a place to eat. A large group of people had gathered in one particular eating-place. The smell of baking bread and freshly cooked fish and chickpeas wafted from the ovens, making everyone's mouth water.

'Where the locals gather, you will find the best

food,' said Halil, leading his men in.

As they sat down and started to tuck into their lunch, they saw Mulla Nasruddin running towards them, thrashing around his arms.

'Mr Speaker,' he said, 'I am so very sorry. I forgot I had asked you to come and see me and I went off to the market to do my shopping.'

Halil and his friends began to laugh. 'But did you see my message on your door?' the speaker asked, looking around at the other customers.

Many of them had heard the men laugh and joke about how they had shamed the Mulla, among them Etki, Kepci and Emir, and were looking on with interest.

'Of course I did,' the Mulla panted. 'Or how would I have known you visited?'

Grinning, Halil drew himself up to his full height and asked loudly, 'Well Mulla, how did you know it was I who visited?'

The Mulla looked embarrassed. He dropped his voice a little. 'Well, Mr Speaker, sir,' he replied. 'How could I not know? You signed your name in big letters across my door.'

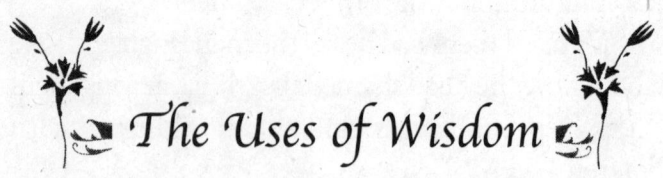

The Uses of Wisdom

Mulla Nasruddin sat in his boat, looking over at the shore for customers. Ferrying people across the river was not the best job he had done by a long way, but it had undoubtedly made him more fit. When he had started, his arms felt as stiff as tree trunks and his back hurt so much that he felt he could not stand at all. Yet, here he was now, as supple and fit as a young man. Not only could he row with the best of them but he could swim like a fish.

Still, the job of ferrying people across the river

was tough. You rowed from one side to the other, then back again—and the money was not all that good. Labourers, the Mulla thought, work the hardest, and they should be paid far more than those who live by their wit. It is all, in the end, about which things we decide to value more. But in this world, it was obviously the brain that was held in higher esteem than the honest sweat of the brow. Quite arbitrary, thought the Mulla, who had tried to earn money in both ways. He knew that physical work was by far harder, though he would never have complained if he was paid handsomely for his wit.

He looked up at the sky. Among the white, fluffy clouds loomed one that was grey and sinister. All around him, the waters reflected its darkness and the waves were growing just that little bit quicker and larger. Not good for the ferryman's trade, at all.

Nasruddin cast a glance towards the shore. There was not a single customer in sight. But wait! Someone seemed to be walking slowly towards the water.

The man reached the water's edge and began looking around for a boat.

'I'm coming,' yelled Nasruddin, loudly, waving his hands to attract the man's attention. 'I'll be there in a moment.'

The man waved back to indicate that he would wait. Nasruddin began rowing with swift, long

strokes, so that his boat glided smoothly forward to the shore.

'*Salam'alaikum, effendi*,' Nasruddin greeted the man. 'Please, let me help you on to my humble vessel.'

The man took Nasruddin's proffered hand and climbed gingerly on to the boat. He ran a hand over the seat and checked his fingertips for evidence of dirt before he sat down.

'Please sit,' Nasruddin spoke briskly, ignoring the insult.

The man sat down and began staring at Nasruddin in a strange way.

Once again, Nasruddin ignored him.

'Excuse me,' the man said at last. 'But you are the famous Mulla Nasruddin, are you not?'

'I am Nasruddin, yes,' replied the Mulla. 'I am not sure about being "famous", though.'

The man continued staring at the Mulla, who continued to ignore him and concentrated on rowing.

'Tell me, what do you think is the reason for your, er, fame?'

'I have no idea,' snapped Nasruddin.

'Is it, perhaps, that you have memorised the Qur'an and are a *hafiz*?'

'I'm afraid that is not the case. I am not a *hafiz*.'

'You are not?' exclaimed the man. 'Then, my friend, you have wasted a quarter of your life!'

Mulla Nasruddin shrugged and gazed into the waves. They were growing larger and stronger. They pushed the boat along with their power.

'Have you read all the great works of grammar?' the man persisted.

Nasruddin shook his head. 'I have not.' It was becoming increasingly difficult to control the boat, so his answers had to be short.

His passenger seemed to be oblivious to the weather. He inhaled deeply. 'I grieve for you,' he sighed. 'You have wasted half your life.'

'We do what we have to do,' Nasruddin replied. 'If we were all learned scholars like yourself, how would the fields yield grain, who would milk the cows, build the roads or make these boats? Each of us has a function—our duty is to fulfill that to the best of our ability.'

The man's expression was disdainful. 'I don't imagine it takes much to learn to row one of these,' he replied.

'Believe me,' muttered Nasruddin. 'It's hard to survive the buffeting of the waves without a few skills. Such as, a certain ability to predict things. Have you any idea how the skies and the waters can change within moments?'

'Are you an astronomer, then?' asked the man. 'Can you predict the weather?'

The Mulla looked up at the sky. Rain was falling fast and furious from fat dark thunderclouds. The boat was rocking dangerously, and water was splashing into it from both sides. 'No. Well no more, anyway, than any other man.'

'Then, Mulla Nasruddin,' the man blurted out, 'you have wasted three-quarters of your life.'

'Can you swim?' Mulla Nasruddin barked. There was at least an inch of water in the boat now.

The man shook his head. 'No, I cannot.'

'In that case,' cried Nasruddin, leaping from the boat. 'You've wasted all your life. This boat is sinking.'

❈ The Honourable Coat ❈

Mulla Nasruddin had been working hard all day.

'Aren't you going to the banquet?' his wife asked as she scrubbed the floor furiously.

'Is it Monday already?' Nasruddin asked, surprised.

'It is,' replied his wife, 'and dinner will be served very soon by the looks of it.'

Nasruddin looked beyond the town square. People had gathered in droves around Ali's house, where the banquet was being held. Now they were moving back, clearing a passage for men carrying large trays of food into the courtyard to lay on the *sofra*, the large tablecloth around which everyone would soon be seated for an excellent and lavish meal.

Nasruddin breathed in. He could smell the *borec* frying, the moist bouquet of herbs and broadbeans with tomatoes and onions streaming through, and above them the mouthwatering aroma of kebabs made from all kinds of meats. There was also the titillating fragrance of piquant sauces that would accompany the food. More enticing than all of those were the yeasty blasts of freshly baked bread that filled the air when the ovens opened to take out the round loaves whose crisp crusts studded with toasted sesame seeds. The bread within was like soft clouds, and would melt as soon as one bit into it.

Nasruddin's mouth was watering. He put down his tools, bid his wife a swift farewell and opened the front door.

'Hoja,' said his wife, pausing in her scrubbing. 'Where are you going?'

'Where do you think I'm going?' Nasruddin replied. 'Can't you hear those aromas calling to me to come and eat?'

'But you're not dressed for a banquet,' said Ayshe.

'A man can't delay his food for the sake of a smart coat,' snapped Nasruddin as he went out of the door and marched across the square as quickly as he could.

Everyone had disappeared into the banquet house by the time he arrived so the Mulla knocked loudly. A man appeared at the door.

'I've come to the banquet,' said Nasruddin.

The man looked him up and down. 'You can't come in dressed like that,' he said rudely. 'You're a disgrace.'

'I'm Mulla Nasruddin. And I have been invited.'

'And I'm Taimur Lang,' barked the man. 'And I rule that you cannot come in.' He banged the door shut in Nasruddin's face.

Nasruddin stared at the door for a moment then spun round and hurried back to his house. Swiftly, he took off his working clothes, had a shower, changed into his formal clothes, put on his fur-trimmed coat and went back across the town square. He knocked at the door of the banquet house again.

The same man answered. But this time he saw Nasruddin's smart coat and behaved very differently.

'Welcome, welcome,' he replied, leading Nasruddin through the hall to a large courtyard in which scores of people sat around a large table. He introduced Nasruddin as an 'honorable guest' and found him a seat at the *sofra*.

Mulla Nasruddin took his seat just as the soup was being served. It was a velvety lentil soup, enriched with spices and delicious vegetables. Great clouds of steam filled the air with a rich perfume.

All the guests dipped their spoons into the soup and raised it to their mouths eagerly. Nasruddin dipped his spoon in with the rest, but instead of bringing the filled spoon to his mouth, he took it to the fur-trimmed collar of his coat. He did this a second time, and a third. The other guests murmured praise of the soup; the Mulla was silent.

'And Hoja? How do *you* rate the soup?' asked Kepci, who was sitting next to him, politely.

Nasruddin shrugged. 'It doesn't matter what I think of the soup,' he replied calmly, as he took a fourth spoon to his collar, and then a fifth.

By now everyone around the table had stopped eating and was staring at Nasruddin.

'Of course it matters,' said Ali. 'You are a guest at our banquet. It matters very much to us what you think of the food.'

'Well,' replied Nasruddin. 'I'm not the guest here, you see. That is why I'm not committing the misdemeanour of eating your wonderful food.'

'But you are, Mulla Nasruddin,' the host insisted. 'You are a most honoured guest.'

'Actually,' retorted Nasruddin, 'the real guest is my honoured coat. For I was not allowed in without it.'

Up and Down

Tap-tap. Bang-bang!

Mulla Nasruddin was hard at work on his roof, fixing the slates to keep out the rain. He was working with as much concentration as he could muster so that he could get this over with as quickly as he could. He wanted to complete everything that had to be done at one go, so that he would not have to come up here again for a very long time. If there was one thing he hated, it was to climb up to this great height and then balance on the top with no reliable protection. He could slip off any time—and if he began to grab at the tiles, he would break those in the process. And Allah have mercy on him, he would have to climb back up again as soon as his bruised flesh and broken bones had mended and start all over again. That, or listen to the scolding of his wife who was always telling him he was lazy, or slow, or foolish, and sat around while she cleaned the house. Lazy? Mulla Nasruddin? No one could ever accuse him of …

'Kind sir!' a voice said urgently.

Nasruddin was startled at the interruption and then very annoyed. That salutation had nearly caused him to lose his balance. 'Who is that?' he asked irritably.

'A stranger, kind sir,' replied the voice.

'Well, what can I do for you?'

'Come down, Hoja, please—and I'll tell you.'

'My friend, do you not see I'm all the way up here, working on the roof of my house?' Nasruddin could hear the annoyance in his own voice and tried to remind himself that patience was a virtue.

'Please sir, I beg you: please come down,' the stranger insisted. 'I have something very important to ask you.'

'Well,' thought Nasruddin, 'I have been so impatient with him, and he still wants to talk to me.

His need must be great. I should go down.'

Carefully, he secured his tools and implements in place so that he would not have to bring them down and carry them up again. Then he began to make his way to the ground, thinking that the scramble down was even more hazardous than the climb up.

Once he had both feet firmly on the ground, he soothed his grazed skin, smoothed his crumpled clothes and ran his hands through his ruffled hair.

The stranger stood looking at him, his hand outstretched.

'What is this important matter you have to discuss?' the Mulla asked.

'Can you spare me some money?'

The Mulla was exasperated. 'I can't believe you brought me all the way down to ask me for money. Am I more likely to have money when I'm on the ground than when I'm on the roof?'

He turned to make the ascent back to the roof.

The man took a quick step forward. 'But sir, what about my request?'

'Follow me,' the Mulla replied wearily, beginning to climb up once again.

The man followed him slowly up. As soon as they were on the roof, he extended his hand again.

Mulla Nasruddin was already delving into his bundle to scrabble around for something.

Several minutes passed. The man remained standing with his palm held out. He cleared his throat meaningfully.

When even more time had elapsed, he spoke again. 'Hoja, have you some money to spare?'

Nasruddin looked up from his bundle with an expression of great surprise. 'No,' he said. 'Of course not.'

'Then why did you bring me all the way up here?'

Nasruddin looked over the edge of the roof. 'Because,' he said, 'you brought me all the way down there, first.'

Upholding the Law

Mulla Nasruddin was walking along when something caught his eye, glittering and gleaming in the street. He bent down and scooped it up.

It was the most gorgeous ring, studded with a huge ruby. Nasruddin slipped it on his finger. It fit perfectly!

'Thank you, God,' Nasruddin said, spreading his hands in prayer. 'What a wonderful present you have sent me.'

All day, he went about his business with a spring

in his step and a tune on his lips. Once in a while, he would stop and look at his wonderful gift. How the stone twinkled at him! How the gold winked as if they were sharing a private joke.

Nasruddin chuckled to himself. 'Oh yes. God is certainly kind to his servant.'

Then suddenly, Mulla Nasruddin stopped chuckling. And he stopped humming and the spring went clean out of his step. He had remembered something.

Just lately, Emperor Taimur Lang had decreed that if something precious was found lying around, then the person who found it had to take it into the marketplace to find its original owner. He had to stand in the market square and ask three times if anyone had lost such an object. If no one claimed it, he was entitled to take it home.

'But I want this ring,' Nasruddin thought. 'It fits my finger. It even speaks to me. Why should I have to return it? How would I know if the true owner is claiming it? Why should it go to someone who gains it by deception?'

As the day went by, Nasruddin became even more outraged at the thought of giving up his ring. He could think of nothing else. By the time he went to bed, his mind was so turbulent that he couldn't sleep. His wife Ayshe, exhausted after a day of furious cleaning, fell asleep as soon as her head touched the pillow. The Mulla listened to her snoring with great annoyance.

At four-thirty in the morning, while the skies were still dark, the Mulla shot out of bed. 'This is no good,' he thought. 'I cannot possibly break Taimur's law. I should complete this business before it is time for the dawn prayer. The law will be observed.'

Quickly, he washed and dressed, put the ring in a small velvet pouch and made his way to the market. When he arrived in the square, the sky had turned a shade lighter and the first rays of light had begun to blur the edges of darkness.

Mulla Nasruddin found a prominent spot in the market square. He mounted a sturdy wooden box and squared his shoulders and began to speak. 'In this box is a ring I found in the street leading to the western entrance of this market. Has anyone lost a ring?'

Mulla Nasruddin waited a few moments for a response. He looked around him. The regular stallholders, who slept in their shops, were only just beginning to stir.

'Has anyone lost a beautiful ring?' he repeated. 'Possibly while coming to the market—or leaving it—on the western street?'

The stallholders were now getting up. Some were

yawning and stretching themselves. The sound of the *shahada* began to fill the marketplace. '*La-ilaha-ill-allah, Muhammadu rasul-allah.*'

Mulla Nasruddin remained silent for a while, in deference to their prayers. He watched as they rose from their beds and made for the public baths to complete their cleansing rituals and be ready to pray as soon as the muezzin's first lines floated through the air. '*Assalaatu khair-um-min anaum.*' Prayer is more beneficial than sleep.

Then Nasruddin asked his question for the third time.

'I found a ring, yesterday in the road leading to the western side of the market. Does anyone claim it?'

A few sleepy-eyed people paused and looked at Mulla Nasruddin. But they quickly decided that he was up to one of his strange antics again and so they went about their business.

Mulla Nasruddin leapt off his wooden box. The spring was most definitely back in his feet, and the hum on his lips. No one had claimed the ring and so now it was legally his.

'Prayer,' he thought, 'is definitely more beneficial that sleep. Why, if I hadn't woken up in time to deal honestly with my duty and in time to say my dawn prayers, I would almost certainly have lost my ring to some greedy claimant.'

The Greater Need

When you stepped out of the mosque and into the street, you could be sure you would come across a beggar or two. Some were so regular that they were almost glued to their chosen spots.

Mulla Nasruddin knew that this was a good place for them to be. After all, people came out from their prayers full of the grace of God and soft with feelings of charity. The beggars took full advantage of this mood.

But nevertheless, when he took two steps out of

the mosque and practically fell over the first beggar's outstretched hands, he was aware of a feeling of great annoyance.

The Mulla was no soft target. 'Are you a big spender?' he asked the man, intending to embarrass him.

'I am,' replied the man, brazen as a brass urn.

'You enjoy sitting around in coffeehouses, telling stories and playing cards?'

'I do!' replied the beggar.

Nasruddin could hardly believe the man's audacity. 'And having a nice dip in the baths every day, no doubt?'

'Couldn't do without it. There's nothing, I say, like a good rub-down in a Turkish bath, to exfoliate the skin and brace you for the day.'

'And no doubt you need a new set of clothes now and then after that luxurious bath?'

'Not now and then, Mulla,' the man objected. 'Frequently.'

The Mulla raised his eyebrows, reached into his pocket and gave the man a small gold coin and moved on, having done his pious act of charity.

Four steps on and he practically trod all over another beggar. This one sat shrunken into his space. There was no extended arm or upturned palm, just a look of meek dejection.

Mulla Nasruddin stopped beside him. 'And you, my man, are you interested in living the good life?'

'The good life?' replied the man. 'All I ask for is a place to sleep and a few morsels of food in my belly.'

'You mean, you don't spend your earnings on fancy meals?'

The man shook his head.

'Or new clothes?'

'No!' replied the second beggar. 'I've already told you. I want to live a life of prayer with enough food to survive on.'

'I'm impressed,' said the Mulla. He reached deep into his pocket and gave the man a small copper coin.

'What!' protested the beggar. 'You gave that profligate there a gold coin—and to me, a devout man, you give only a meagre copper coin?'

The Mulla frowned. 'But surely you understand,' he said. 'His need is far greater than yours.'

Where There Is Light

Late in the evening—it was dark, and the air had started to go crunchy—Mulla Nasruddin was scrabbling around on the ground, searching. As he searched beneath a streetlight, he mumbled to himself.

'What are you looking for, Hoja?' asked Ali, stopping to help.

'My ring,' muttered the Mulla. 'I've lost my ring.'

'Where do you think you dropped it?' Ali asked.

'In my basement,' the Mulla replied without hesitation.

Ali stepped back in surprise. 'Then why, Mulla, are you not looking in your basement?'

Now it was the Mulla's turn to be surprised. 'It's far too dark in my basement. I'm looking where there's some light to see by.'

Tricking the Mulla

One sunny day, two boys were playing beneath a cypress tree when they suddenly saw a small bird. Mehmet sprang forward swiftly and caught the bird.

Yusuf was taken aback. 'How did you do that?' he asked.

Mehmet shrugged and replied, as little boys do, 'I don't know. Just did it.'

'What will you do with it now?'

Mehmet shrugged again. 'Don't know. What do you think we should do?' He could feel the small creature flapping about in his palms.

'I know,' Yusuf cried out. 'Let's play a trick on Mulla Nasruddin.'

Mehmet grinned cheekily. 'That's a brilliant idea. How will we do that?'

Both boys fell silent for a while, thinking what kind of trick to play on the Mulla.

'I know!' said Mehmet at last. 'I'll hold out my palms and I'll ask, "Hoja, hoja, I'm holding something in my hands. Can you tell if it is alive or dead?"'

'He'll easily guess that,' replied Yusuf. 'He's far too clever not to know the answer to that.'

Mehmet shook his head. 'I have a trick up my sleeve.'

'Well, what is it? If he says it's alive, we lose.'

Mehmet shook his head again. 'No, no, no. You don't understand. If he says the bird is dead, I'll let it fly away...'

'Yes, but what if he says it's alive?'

'Simple,' replied Mehmet, 'it's so tiny, I'll crush it my palms and it will be dead. So you see, either way, we'll win.'

Yusuf did not like the idea of a small bird being killed for a joke, even if it was to get the better of the Mulla. But he went along with his friend, praying hard that the Mulla would guess that the bird was dead.

They made their way towards the Mulla's house. As they approached, they saw him walking very briskly up an incline in the opposite direction.

'Mulla, Mulla,' shouted the boys. 'Please, stop. We need to ask you a question.'

The Mulla stopped. 'Well, hurry up,' he called back. 'I've work to do, you know.'

The boys broke into a run. When they reached him, Mehmet held out his hands with the bird enclosed.

The Mulla saw their cheeky grins and knew at once that they wanted to play a trick on him.

'See my hands, Hoja,' began Mehmet.

'Well, you're holding your hands right in front of me, so if I couldn't see them, I would have to be blind, wouldn't I?' said the Mulla crustily. But he was smiling inside.

'Okay,' said the boy. 'So, can you tell me—this thing I'm holding in my hand, is it alive or dead?'

'Is that not in your hands?' replied the Mulla.

Mehmet stopped. Did the Mulla know what he had in mind? A little less certainly, he said, 'You always ask questions in answer to questions, Hoja.'

The Mulla looked him right in the eye. 'Is that so?'

The Fruit of the Tree

It was a very hot and sunny day.

Today of all days, Mulla Nasruddin had found work loading large bags of grain from his employer's storerooms on to waiting donkeys and carts. The sun was burning through his scarf and his hair until his scalp felt as if it was on fire, and he was pouring with sweat. But he carried on, dragging and loading one bag after another until finally he had finished. 'Praise Allah,' he gasped, and set off to make his way back to his town.

On the way he came across a field. It looked peaceful and a soft breeze was blowing. Nasruddin looked around him, enjoying the breeze and feasting his eyes on the luscious greenery around him. He decided to pause a while in this resting room that God had provided. His gaze came to rest on a tall tree. Its branches spread out, creating a cool, shady space beneath.

'That's where I shall lie down,' Mulla decided, walking towards the tree at a leisurely pace.

As he drew nearer, he saw that the tree was studded with walnuts, small, brown and textured with wonderful patterns. He resolved that after he had rested, he would fill a bag with walnuts and take them home to his wife. Perhaps, if Ayshe could find some time in between her bouts of cleaning, she would turn them into delicious delicacies for their dinner.

Nasruddin lay down on the grass, beneath the shade of the walnut tree, thanking God for all he saw around him. His eyes were drawn to a piece of foliage nearby. Some enormous pumpkins appeared to be growing right out of the ground.

The Mulla raised himself on one arm and gazed in wonder at the massive vegetables. 'Good heavens,' he thought. 'Such gigantic pumpkins—and they're growing on those fragile, creeping vines!'

Nasruddin looked up at the tree above him and

the tiny walnuts that adorned this magnificent tree with its spreading habit, and back again at the pumpkins.

'I cannot for the life of me work out what lies behind the mysterious ways of nature!' he thought. 'That such a huge, strong tree should produce such tiny fruit while a frail, thin creeper produces such a mammoth!'

As he pondered, his weariness caught up with him. The enigma slipped into the deeper recesses of his mind; his eyelids grew heavy and fluttered shut.

Clunk!

The Mulla leaped up in shock, rubbing a sore spot on his forehead as he sat looking around indignantly to find the culprit. 'Who's throwing stones at me? Come out, show yourself!'

Clunk!

This time, the hit was on the crown of his head.

The Mulla looked up to see who was hiding in the branches of the tree. There was no one he could see.

Then, slowly, his eyes focussed on the walnuts. His hand felt around on the grass behind him. Two walnuts.

Nasruddin scrambled out from under the tree and held his hands up to the skies.

'*Al-hamdu-lillah*! Praise God who is all-knowing,

all-wise!' he cried out. 'The walnut has only given me a bit of a knock! If you had put a pumpkin in its place, I would not have been standing up right now, thanking you!'

The End of the World

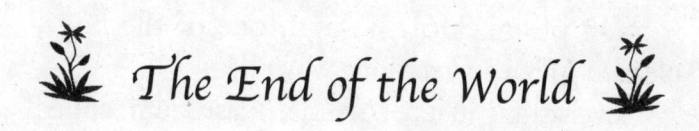

Mulla Nasruddin saw a healthy young sheep in the market.

'I'll buy it now,' he thought, 'while it is still cheap. After a few months of good feeding on the summer grass, it'll produce enough wool to make into something useful for the winter, and twice the quantity of meat—and what's more it will be sweet and tender from the meadow grass.'

He walked along dreaming about the wonderful dishes he could make from the animal in due course and who he would invite to share in his feast.

Suddenly, a voice broke into his thoughts.

'What-what-what?' The Mulla looked around, slightly dazed, as if he had been woken from a deep sleep.

'Can we come and eat your sheep with you?'

Nasruddin looked at half-a-dozen upturned faces and a dozen eyes brimming over with mischief.

The Mulla smiled. 'Of course, of course,' he said. 'But it will be a few months yet.'

'Oh please, Hoja,' Yusuf, one of the boys, pleaded. 'That's a very long way off.'

'Everything in its own time,' Nasruddin replied firmly. 'Would you eat a melon before it is ripe?'

'But Hoja, we want to eat it tonight.'

'No,' the Mulla said, walking on. 'Everything has its own season. You must learn to wait.'

'But Hoja,' called the boys running after him. 'Please listen.'

'What is it now? I have work to do, you know.'

'What is the point of waiting?' demanded Mehmet, another boy. 'Haven't you heard?'

'Heard what?'

'The world is coming to an end tonight.'

Mulla Nasruddin stopped walking. 'Is that a fact?' he said.

The boys nodded eagerly.

'In that case,' said the Mulla. 'I will cook the sheep this afternoon. And you are all invited. Meet me by the river in two hours and we will have a great feast.'

Two hours later when Mulla Nasruddin arrived at the river with his sheep following behind him on a rope, the boys were already waiting eagerly. They were flushed and sweaty from walking in the sun, but excited at the prospect of the feast they would soon be devouring!

'Well now,' the Mulla said. 'I have to prepare the beast and set him to cook. That will all take a while. Why don't you lads take a swim while I get to work? Then you can join the rest of the guests in time for the meal.'

The boys thought this was a good idea. The sun was high in the sky and it would be pleasant to cool off. They took off their shirts and trousers, and plunged in.

The Mulla went about his work, listening to the boys splashing about in the water, and absorbed in all kinds of games. It was not long before he had a roaring fire going and the lamb barbecuing on the spit. The aroma of the cooking meat wafted towards the town, past the boys in the river, alerting everyone that the meal would soon be ready.

The boys stopped messing about and swam purposefully to the river bank to get dressed and get their share of the feast before any of the other guests arrived. But when they reached the bank, there was an unforeseen problem. Their clothes were missing! They looked around but there was no sign of them. They swam up and down several yards, thinking the clothes might have been blown along the river. But there was no sign of them.

'Hoja!' they yelled. 'Have you seen our clothes?'

'I have,' the Mulla replied.

'Where are they? We need them.'

'The world's coming to an end today,' replied Nasruddin, looking a little puzzled. 'So I used them for my fire. I didn't think you'd need them.'

Let the Turban Speak

Emir, his neighbour, stopped Mulla Nasruddin one day as he was setting off on some work.

'Hoja, please, will you read this letter for me?'

'I am very busy today,' the Mulla replied. 'Go to the mosque and you will surely find an *aalim* there to read it for you.'

'Please, Hoja,' Emir begged. 'The *aalim* in the mosque will charge me money and I don't want to pay. I know you will do it for free.'

'Give it to me then,' said the Mulla. He opened

the letter, stretched it out, smoothed away the wrinkles and looked carefully at the script. But though he could recognise a letter of the alphabet here and there, he could not decipher any of the words.

'I'm very sorry, friend,' he said at last. 'But I can't make out a single one of these words.'

Emir was angry. 'In that case, you don't deserve to wear that turban!' he shouted. 'Because you bring disgrace to it.'

Immediately, Nasruddin took off his turban. 'Here,' he said, 'you take it. And may it help you to read.'

Strange Town, Strange Ways

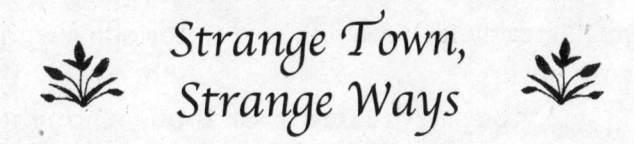

It was a bitter day, with an icy wind that prised its fingers into Mulla Nasruddin's collar and down his back. He shuddered, pulling his coat tighter around his neck. As he walked on, each step felt heavier than the last. He had never been to this town before and he would not be here now, were it not for some important business. Keeping his mind firmly on the business ahead, he breathed deeply and walked on.

'I've survived this kind of situation before,' he

reminded himself. 'I'll do it again.'

In the distance, he saw some twinkling lights and smelt the familiar fragrance of a mouthwatering bean casserole. With renewed strength, he propelled himself towards the inn. Visions of sitting by the fire with a large plate of food in front of him urged him on.

'Grrr! Woof!'

Nasruddin was snapped out of his reverie. Between him and his fantasy stood a large, brown dog. Its eyes glowed in the dimming evening light and its great fangs were yellowed and dripping with slimy saliva.

'He, too, is dreaming of food,' thought Nasruddin. 'But *I* am his food. And if I don't do something about it, he'll achieve his wish instead of me achieving mine.'

The dog was running towards him now. Swiftly, Nasruddin dropped to the ground to pick up a stone. But the stone would not budge. It was encased in a covering of ice and stuck solidly to the ground. The Mulla decided it was futile to try to get it loose. Gathering up his coat and shawl, he jumped on to a high ledge out of the brute's reach.

Some people had come out of the inn now and were calming down the dog.

Nasruddin felt irritable. 'What kind of hospitality

is this?' he snapped, as some men tried to help him down. 'You tether your rocks and let your dogs run free.'

❦ Fair Exchange ❦

There was a knock on the door. Mulla Nasruddin hurried to respond.

Outside, stood a well-dressed, middle-aged man.

The Mulla bowed his head in greeting. Being too polite to ask directly who he was and what he wanted, he waited for the man to state his business.

'May I have the honour of speaking to the great Mulla Nasruddin?' inquired the man.

'Your humble servant,' replied Nasruddin. 'I am Nasruddin. But I'm not at all sure that I am great in anyway.'

The man bowed respectfully. 'I have made a long detour to meet you, *effendi*,' he said. 'My name is Iskender. I have travelled far and wide in search of knowledge, and I have often heard people mention you in one connection or another.'

'I really don't know why,' replied Nasruddin. 'But let me, at least, invite you into my humble home, so that you can refresh yourself and have a little rest.'

Iskender accepted gratefully. He had a wash and relaxed over some refreshments and several cups of fresh mint tea while the Mulla went about his business, occasionally stopping to inquire if there was anything he wanted, or sitting down to have a brief chat. His wife Ayshe was in the back room, cleaning all the windows with soap and water.

Iskender was a scholar and a moralist who travelled the world to discover the rules and regulations that bind different societies and the way in which they behaved. Manners, this man told Nasruddin, were the essence of civilisation.

Nasruddin was not sure he agreed but the matter did not interest him enough to argue. Besides, Ayshe had set him a long list of tasks to be completed before the time of the *zuhar* prayer.

The scholar dozed off for a while. When he awoke and had a wash, the Mulla asked if he would like to accompany him to the mosque for the *zuhar* prayers.'

'Of course,' replied Iskender.

So Nasruddin led him to the mosque, talking on the way about this and that—or rather, listening, while the scholar laid down the law about modes of behaviour, how people should conduct themselves and even how they should think.

Nasruddin walked faster and faster, hoping the man would get short of breath and stop talking. But no such luck.

The Mulla enjoyed saying his prayers but on this occasion, he was elated to arrive in the great prayer courtyard and spread out his *musalla* and enjoy a few moments of peace.

After prayers, the Mulla exchanged greetings with a number of people and introduced them to his eminent guest. And when the socialising was over, he began to wonder how much longer the scholar expected to be entertained.

'My friend,' said Iskender, as if he could read Nasruddin's mind, 'I must not take up too much more of your time. But in exchange for your hospitality and your excellent conversation, I would like to take you to a good eating place. Then, with your permission, I will be on my way.'

'My conversation?' Nasruddin thought. 'What

conversation? I couldn't get a word out of my mouth. You delivered one monologue after another!'

But he was never one to turn down the chance of a good meal, so he kept his own counsel. He led the scholar to a restaurant famous for its fresh fish.

The two men sat down at a comfortable table and placed their order.

'Both of you want fish?'

The men nodded.

'The same kind of fish?'

'Yes,' growled Iskender. 'And make it quick.'

'Cooked in the same way?'

'Fried, with all the special bits and pieces you serve every time I come,' said Nasruddin.

The man nodded and went away.

'I once read a superb treatise on the principles of good service,' began the scholar. 'Perhaps I should let this man have the benefit of my knowledge. It says clearly that...'

Nasruddin groaned inwardly, making up his mind to track down the villains who made it their business to spread vicious rumours about his superior wisdom that brought men such as this self-opinionated, puffed-up braggart to ruin his day. In fact, he was just wondering if he should get up and run all the way home, when the whiff of his frying fish wafted to and fro, delicately, playfully, bumping his nose, receding, returning. And following behind it, the proprietor, holding aloft a tray and two empty plates.

With a flourish, he set down the two plates and then the platter with its delectable rim of crisp green salad, studded with red pepper, tomatoes and chickpeas. In the middle, lay two succulent fish, whole and plump, as if they had leapt directly from the sea to land in the frying pan. And how beautiful they looked, one large fish and one much smaller one, nestling side by side.

Iskender was still in the middle of his diatribe. Without interrupting his flow, Nasruddin reached out and transferred the larger fish to his own plate.

The scholar gasped and spluttered so loudly that his words got stuck in his throat. Nasruddin had to cover the platter with his arms to prevent the scholar's spit from contaminating the food.

'I cannot believe it!' the man gasped when he could finally shut his mouth. 'You have just violated every one of even the most basic ethics known to man.'

'Why do you say that?' Nasruddin asked and immediately wished he had kept his mouth shut for now the man was spewing out the name of every book of ethics and exemplar of manners that he could remember.

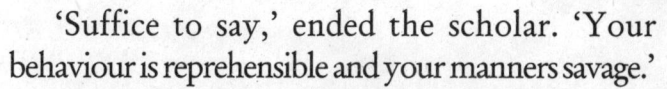

'Suffice to say,' ended the scholar. 'Your behaviour is reprehensible and your manners savage.'

'In that case, sir,' said Nasruddin, desperate to start eating his fish while it was still hot, 'tell me what you would have done.'

'I, sir,' said Iskender, 'having regard to manners and culture, and being a civilised man, would have given you the larger fish and insisted on eating the smaller one myself.'

Nasruddin smiled happily and pushed forward the platter.

'Then, sir, it will be exactly as you wish. Here is the smaller fish.'

❋ The Eternal Duck ❋

It was a long summer's day, and very hot.

Mulla Nasruddin had worked hard all day and he felt weary. But he was also content that the work had been done, and done well.

He opened his front door and looked out at the hills that formed a distant circle around his small town. The heat haze was beginning to lift. Nasruddin listened to the evening breeze rustling through the green, shiny leaves of the cypress trees. He felt relaxed.

Suddenly, there was a new sound disrupting the whisper of the wind and the soft chattering of birds: clonk, clonk, clonk. The sound was getting louder, as if it was coming towards him.

The Mulla stepped out into the street. He craned his neck, peering in the direction of the sound.

And there it was ... a pair of sturdy boots. Its owner was plodding determinedly towards Nasruddin's house, bearing a heavy load across both shoulders on a rod.

'I know that man!' thought Nasruddin, mentally peeling off the years from the stranger to see how he would have looked in his youth.

'My brother, Nasruddin!' the man exclaimed.

Nasruddin recognised him now. 'My uncle's son, Esed,' he responded equally enthusiastically.

His cousin dropped his burden and flung his arms around the Mulla. 'It has been too long.'

'Too long indeed,' replied Nasruddin. 'And how are things in Sivrihisar?'

'The place of your birth is the same as ever. Your relatives think of you often. Of course we hear all the time about your fame and wisdom.'

'Ahhh! All exaggeration and nonsense,' Nasruddin said, modest as ever.

'We thought so, too,' Esed agreed. 'You seem to us no different than any other person in Sivrihisar.'

Nasruddin nodded. 'We are an exceptional people, a unique people.'

Esed looked a bit bemused and very tired.

'But what are we standing outside for when we could be sitting comfortably inside? Come in, brother. Come and refresh yourself, then we'll have something to eat.'

Gratefully, Esed followed Nasruddin into the house and out again through the back to the bathhouse.

While Esed was having a shower, Nasruddin could hear another strange noise. It seemed to be a day for unusual sounds. Squawking? No, not quite. Quacking? That was it. Definitely quacking.

'I'll find out soon enough,' Nasruddin thought, going into the kitchen to put together some food for his cousin. Ayshe was busy cleaning the floor with soap and a wooden brush. She could not be interrupted when she was cleaning, so the Mulla prepared some refreshing mint tea. He also flavoured a cool bowl of yoghurt with some dill and assembled a fine selection of crunchy vegetables. By this time, Esed had emerged from the shower.

The Mulla placed a steaming dish of meat casserole on the table. Then he flung out his arms and spoke in a commanding voice, so that he could drown out the quacking noise outside. 'Eat! Please eat.'

Esed didn't wait for a second invitation. He plunged straight into the meal.

By the time they had both eaten and sat sipping their tea, Nasruddin had begun to worry about the noise. Esed had not once remarked on the periodic quacks that had gone on through supper. The Mulla was beginning to wonder if there was something wrong with his ears—or even his mind.

'Do you hear a noise, brother?' he asked.

'A noise? What kind of a noise?' Esed was puzzled.

Nasruddin grew anxious. 'A kind of ... quacking.'

Esed burst out laughing. He jumped to his feet and rushed out. A few moments later, he came back in, holding up the fattest, biggest duck Mulla Nasruddin had ever seen.

'A small gift for you to enjoy after I'm gone,' Esed said smiling.

Nasruddin was delighted. A duck was a rare treat. And this was a big one. He was also hugely relieved to discover that the noises were not in his head.

The next morning, after Esed left, Nasruddin cooked the duck and invited Ali, Salih, Kepic and other friends to a meal. It was greatly enjoyed by everyone.

They were still talking about the feast when the

sun set on the last evenings of summer and rose again in its autumn incarnation. And then, in the middle of autumn as the Mulla stood gazing at the bronzing leaves still clinging to the branches and at the yellow ones raining down on the grass to create golden lakes, he heard the tramp, tramp, tramp of stout travelling boots.

Another traveller appeared, carrying a heavy burden. He, too, came up to Nasruddin, but this time, the Mulla did not recognise him.

'I am a cousin of the relative who brought you the duck,' he said. 'I wonder if I might stay with you for the night.'

'Of course,' said Nasruddin, opening his door wide.

And as the man went to wash, the Mulla got to work preparing him a meal. Ayshe was determinedly cleaning the cupboards today. And when the man had eaten and drunk and had a good night's sleep, he thanked the Mulla profusely and went on his way.

The Mulla, who had been waiting to receive his duck, was a little disappointed but he gave himself a telling off. 'For shame, Nasruddin. Hospitality is your duty. You must not expect thanks in kind.'

Autumn gave way to winter and the colder days brought more travellers wanting hospitality from Nasruddin. They were relatives of Esed. And friends of the relatives of Esed, and friends of friends of Esed. And their friends, too. They all mentioned Esed and his generous gift and Nasruddin felt obliged to acknowledge the gift of the duck.

'Ah!' the Mulla would laugh. 'It's that noisy duck again. Would you believe how its quack has resounded all over the country!'

So, Nasruddin would invite in the visitors and feed them—but never again did a single one of them bring with him a duck, or a chicken, or even a tiny bird.

Winter was always hard and food was often scarce. But Nasruddin remained true to his decision and gave away the best he had. He would kill one of his decreasing flocks of chickens, make a hearty stew and feed his guests.

As winter progressed, the travellers kept coming. The meals dwindled from hearty chicken stew to thin chicken stew to even thinner chicken soup.

And then came another guest.

'And who are you?' Nasruddin asked.

'Well, I know a man who knew someone whose relative's friend knew a woman who married a man who once travelled through Sivrihisar and heard of a man who ...'

'Come in,' said Nasruddin and sent the man out for his wash. He soon came back in, rolled up his sleeves and prepared to tuck into his food.

Mulla Nasruddin placed a bowl of warm water before him.

'This doesn't look to me like duck stew,' the visitor said.

'Let me explain,' began Nasruddin. 'You know the duck my cousin Esed brought? Well, this is the soup of its soup of its soup of its soup of ...'

🌼 The Runaway Basket 🌼

Mulla Nasruddin loved going to the market, whether it was to eat, sell something, stand on a wooden crate and give advice or, as he sometimes did, to ask for money. But today he was there to shop and that was one of his favourite pastimes. He loved looking at the gleaming, purple aubergines, stroking the bright, red tomatoes and picking out the freshest, most tender beans. He liked to smell aromatic mint leaves; sniff bunches of parsley and select the finest of feathery fronded dill. And then there was the fruit section and over on the other side, cuts of meat, clean and succulent. And of course there were all the things that were not for eating at all.

He went along, enjoying himself to the full. He picked up a handful of plums here and a piece of melon there; some essence of roses from the *attar*; a few pastries so crisp and so airy that they would have flown off had they not been weighted down with finely ground almonds and soaked in honey. After he had wandered around the stalls for a while, he became a little tired, what with chatting and snacking and picking things up and dropping them into his basket.

'My pocket is light now,' he thought. 'And my basket is very heavy. It's time to go home.'

Nasruddin felt around in his pocket and found enough money to pay a porter.

'My good man,' he said, spotting a strong young fellow. 'Will you carry my basket home for me?'

'That's what I'm here for, *effendi*,' the man replied.

After a little haggling, they agreed upon a fee. 'You drive a hard bargain,' Nasruddin grumbled. 'If a man hired you for a whole day, he'd be bankrupt.'

Nasruddin told him where he was going; the man picked up the basket and off they went. Soon the market was behind them.

As they walked along the bare, deserted stretch,

Nasruddin slowed down. The young man, however, kept up a steady, swift pace and was putting more and more distance between himself and the Mulla.

'The young don't realise how lucky they are to have such energy,' the Mulla thought, recalling his younger days. 'What I would give to have some of that stamina back!'

As he watched, the man broke into a run. After a few yards, he leapt off the track and into the scrub.

'Wait! Hey! Young man!' shouted Nasruddin. 'You're going the wrong way.'

But the man knew exactly where he was going and it was not to Nasruddin's house.

The Mulla had a bad week. He had spent all his money and passed the next seven days scrounging around for whatever he could find in his larder. Fortunately, his wife Ayshe had not cleaned the cupboards for a few days so there were still some odds and ends left. They survived on rations of chickpeas, *burghul* and a few herbs and vegetables from the garden and the charity of neighbours. Of course, everyone had heard all about the porter and what he had done. And so between prayer and self-reproach—and several trips to the market to try to earn some money—the week elapsed. It was market day for Nasruddin again.

Armed with a new basket, Nasruddin strode into

the market. It was a smaller basket because he wanted to make sure he would not load it up with more stuff than he could carry himself. And as he strolled along the stores, he stopped here and there for a chat and a laugh.

'Hoja,' Salih hissed, interrupting him in mid-sentence. 'Look there. That's the man who stole your basket.'

Nasruddin looked up. It was the man who had run off with his shopping.

The Mulla flung himself behind a stall.

Salih looked around, bewildered. One moment the Mulla was there, the next he was gone.

He looked around and finally saw Nasruddin cowering behind a cartload of vegetables.

'What are you doing?' asked Salih.

'Hiding, of course,' Nasruddin snapped. 'What do you think I'm doing?'

Salih was incredulous. 'But why are you hiding?'

'That porter has been carrying my basket for a week,' said Nasruddin. 'A week's wages are more than the basket was worth.'

New Clothes

Mulla Nasruddin decided to buy some new clothes.

He had exacting standards and he only bought clothes once a year in Ramadan, in keeping with the *sunna*, so he was determined to find quality goods. He would buy only well-cut, well-stitched clothes made from robust fabric that would last for a good, long time.

At last he came to a shop that met with his approval.

He walked in and looked around at the clothes on display, feeling the fabric, checking out the stitching by giving it a pull and tug.

When he finally saw something he liked, he walked over to the shopkeeper and pointed to a pair of trousers. 'Can you show me those,' he said. 'I want to try them on.'

'Of course, *effendi*,' the shopkeeper said, jumping up to serve him.

Nasruddin tried on the trousers. Then he took them off, folded them neatly and handed them back to the shopkeeper.

'I've changed my mind,' he said. 'I spotted a very smart coat while I was trying these on. I think I would prefer to buy that.'

The shopkeeper was used to people changing their minds. He didn't care what the customer bought, so long as he made a sale. He brought the coat over and handed it to Nasruddin.

'What's the price of this?' Nasruddin asked as he tried it on.

'The same as the trousers,' replied the shopkeeper.

Nasruddin tried on the coat, squared his shoulders, swung his arms about, buttoned up the jacket and made sure he was quite comfortable.

'I will keep this coat,' he said. He picked up his old coat and walked out of the shop.

'*Effendi*, please wait!' the shopkeeper called out, running out after him.

Nasruddin stopped. 'What's the matter?' he asked.

'Forgive me, *effendi* but ... you haven't paid for the coat, *effendi*,' said the shopkeeper.

Nasruddin was irritated. 'Of course, I haven't,' he said. 'You told me it was the same price as the trousers I returned.'

The man stopped for a moment, puzzled. 'You didn't pay for the trousers, either, *effendi*.'

'Well, why on earth would I pay for something I never bought?'

Dying to Keep

Mulla Nasruddin and his friends were on their way back to their small town. They chatted and laughed and teased each other as they walked along. Today, Husnu seemed to be the butt of most jokes.

'You're probably the wealthiest among us,' the others teased. 'Why don't you ever invite us to your house for a feast?'

Husnu hedged. 'I'm ashamed of my wife's cooking. I will be a disgrace in the entire town if I throw a feast.'

'My wife will help prepare the feast,' said Kepci. 'You know how well she cooks.'

'I wouldn't dream of putting her to the trouble. Besides, it would be an insult to my wife.'

'Well then, the only solution is for you to take us all out to a meal,' laughed Salih.

The ribbing continued.

Nasruddin lagged behind a bit, feeling sorry for the man. A man who hoarded his wealth and lived with such meanness of spirit was worse than someone who lived in genuine poverty. He was to be pitied. The man needed to be helped, not tormented.

The teasing increased as they approached the river that ran alongside their town.

'Forget about the feast,' Kepci was saying. 'You can surely lend me some money for my daughter's wedding?'

Husnu became so flustered that he broke away from the crowd of laughing friends. In his annoyance, he failed to notice where he was going and his foot slid in the slippery mud of the river bank.

The next moment, he had fallen into the river.

His friends stood back, laughing, as Husnu thrashed his arms in the water. The current of the water was swift. As they watched Husnu flounder, it slowly dawned on them that he could not swim.

'He's drowning!' shouted Nasruddin, who had

been walking some way behind. 'Save him someone, quick.'

Immediately, Kepci flung himself to the ground and stretched out his arm.

'Give me your hand,' he shouted. 'I'll pull you out.'

Husnu seemed to hear but he made no attempt to stretch out his arm. His friends watched, terrified, as he sank below the surface of the water.

A second later, he reappeared spluttering. Salih put out his arm, now, calling out, 'Give me your hand, my friend. Let me pull you out.'

Again, Husnu ignored the offer as he thrashed about.

His friends were filled with regret. 'We went too far with our teasing,' Kepci said remorsefully. 'He'd rather die than accept our help.'

Mulla Nasruddin had caught up with the group by now. He walked to the edge of the water and stretched out his arm. 'My friend,' he called. 'Here is my hand. Please take it.'

Immediately, Husnu reached out and took Nasruddin's hand.

'It is because you stayed out of the teasing,' Salih said, feeling ashamed. 'If you had been part of it, we would have lost a friend today.'

'The difference was in the offer,' replied

Nasruddin. 'Instead of asking for his hand, I offered him mine. He is never willing to give, but was happy, as usual, to take.'

The Life of a Pot

Someone had borrowed his large pot from Mulla Nasruddin but had never returned it. The Mulla hadn't bothered too much about it.

But today, he desperately needed a large pot to prepare a meal for his guests.

'I know,' he thought, 'I'll borrow one from my neighbour Emir. He and his family will be joining me for the meal, which means they will not be cooking tonight.'

So he went along to his neighbour and asked to

borrow the pot. He brought it home and spent the afternoon cooking. That night his guests ate a marvellous meal.

The following day, true to his word, Nasruddin washed out the pot and took it back to Emir.

'Thank you so much,' the Mulla said. 'I don't know what I would have done if you had not helped me out.' With a twinkle in his eye, he popped the pot down. As it hit the ground, there was a clink.

'What was that clanging noise?' Emir asked.

Mulla Nasruddin smiled. 'It sounds as if there might be something inside,' he replied. 'We'd better have a look.'

He tipped the pot on its side and peered inside. And there, sitting neatly in the womb of the large pot was another one almost exactly like it, but quite a bit smaller.

'Goodness,' exclaimed Emir. 'I wonder where that came from?'

'Your pot had a baby, how else can we explain it?' said Nasruddin.

Nasruddin resolved to find the man who had borrowed his pot. He did not want to be caught short again.

But of course, with something or the other always on his mind and so many chores and the business of living, he kept putting it off until he found himself in exactly the situation he had wanted to avoid.

So, there he was again: another feast to cook and another occasion when he would have to go to his neighbour, fez in hand, to borrow his pot. Emir would think him a terrible nuisance. But, of course, he had to ask, so ask he did. And Emir showed less grace than the first time.

The meal was cooked, and the guests were all well fed.

The very next morning, before he had time to return the pot, Nasruddin was called away from the town on urgent business. He consoled himself that his neighbour had not planned for any feast in the next day or two, so he could do without his big pot.

When he returned a few days later, Emir came immediately and knocked on the door to ask for his pot.

The Mulla was tired and hungry and also a little offended by Emir's behaviour. Did the man think he was going to run away with his mighty pot?

'Where's my pot?' Emir demanded.

'It died,' replied Nasruddin, irritably.

'Pots can't die,' Emir retorted. 'I don't believe you.'

Nasruddin looked him in the eye. 'Then how is it you believe they can give birth?'

The Rules of the Game

Market day came. Nasruddin hobbled along to the central street and placed himself in a busy spot, waiting for passers-by to drop a coin in his outstretched hand. Over time, many had developed a funny little game. They would offer him a large coin and a small coin, and ask him to choose.

'Take your pick, Hoja,' they would say.

The Mulla was no fool. Nor was he greedy. 'I'll take this, and may the blessings of God be with you,' he would say, selecting the smaller coin.

One after the other, the men would put the larger coin back in their pockets and go on their way, laughing and chortling. Week after week, they would return to play the game with Nasruddin, for the cost of a small coin was nothing in return for the big laugh Nasruddin's foolishness afforded them.

Each week, the queues grew longer, and the laughing was prolonged. The Mulla stuck to his principle, reacting amiably to the men laughing at him. Pride, after all, was something he had struggled to get rid of. And, indeed, apart from the need to make a little money in hard times, his aim was to keep pride in its place and strengthen humility. If his actions made people laugh, well, what was wrong with that?

One day, a passing stranger saw the line of men stretching out in front of Mulla Nasruddin and stopped to watch what was going on. One after the other, the men in the queue placed two coins in their hands and asked Nasruddin to choose. Each time he chose the smaller coin, and everyone in the queue burst into laughter.

Nasruddin looked unperturbed. Hadn't the Prophet himself, peace be upon him, said that God smiled on those who brought a smile to the face of others?

The man joined the queue. At last, his turn came and he stood facing Nasruddin. He stretched out a palm in which was placed a single gold coin.

Without hesitation, Nasruddin picked it up and thanked the man.

'I can see that you are not a greedy man,' said the stranger, 'but it must be humiliating to stand here day after day, with people laughing at your modesty. You should take the larger coin.'

'What you say is true,' Nasruddin replied, 'and I'm grateful for your advice. But these men come here to laugh at my foolishness. If I break the rules of the game, I would be the bigger fool!'

The Donkey's Load

'Oi Mulla!' the officer at the checkpost called out to Nasruddin as he trudged across the border with his donkeys.

'What do you want now?' Nasruddin asked. 'I've had a long, tiring day. Let me go home, eat my dinner and sleep.'

The officer came right up close to Nasruddin and glowered at him. 'You stop now! And do as I say.'

The Mulla stopped.

'What are your donkeys carrying?' the officer

asked.

Nasruddin sighed. 'The same load as every other day,' he sighed.

'Yes, and what's that?' demanded the officer.

'Straw. Just ordinary, harmless straw.'

'Lift it off the donkey's back.'

'For heaven's sake!' the Mulla snapped. 'What do you think you're going to find?'

The officer raised his truncheon. 'Do as I say.'

Nasruddin flinched. 'Okay, okay. As you say. But I swear to you there is nothing illegal in any of those bags.'

Nasruddin was thoroughly annoyed with the officer but he decided it would be less painful to lift down his bundle than to be beaten with a truncheon. So he dragged down the saddlebags and stood back, watching, as the officer prodded and poked the contents until they were strewn all over the ground.

Finally, the officer stepped away with an angry cry. 'I know you are smuggling something. I swear I will find out one day!'

'And are you going to help me pick up my goods, this time?' Nasruddin snorted.

The official raised his truncheon and ran at Nasruddin in fury and frustration. Nasruddin, never one to risk pain except for a very good reason, made a swift decision to leave.

Nothing changed. The weeks changed into months, the months to years, Mulla Nasruddin crossed the same checkpost week in and week out, and the officers turned out his goods, usually straw and other such simple products, trying to expose him as a smuggler.

'Why,' Nasruddin would ask them again and again, 'don't you give up?'

And sometimes the officers were so furious, they would set his products alight to find the contraband.

'What are you hoping to find?' Nasruddin would challenge. 'My donkeys are not smuggling anything.'

And they would douse his goods in tubs of water, hoping for something illegal to float to the top.

'You are looking in the wrong place,' Nasruddin would say. 'You should ask your informants what I'm supposed to be smuggling.'

All the years that Nasruddin travelled through that checkpost, backwards and forwards with his donkeys, the officers found nothing.

'Why don't you give up?' the Mulla asked, repeatedly.

'Because,' answered the officials, gritting their teeth, 'we can see that you are getting richer year by year. And it cannot be from selling straw.'

Finally, Nasruddin decided one day that he had enough money to stop trading. It had been a hard few years, made more difficult by officials.

And so, Nasruddin retired and began to live a more restful life. He worked in the community and advised people on legal matters; he even became a judge. In the course of time, he became highly respected. His wife Ayshe had a larger house to clean. Even the sultan sent for him when he needed counsel.

One day, as he came through the palace gates, a man hurried up to him.

'Mulla!' he called, 'Oh Mulla Nasruddin.'

Nasruddin recognised one of the officials from the checkpost who had given him such trouble all those years ago.

'You!' he said. 'What do you want to search me for now? Do you think I've stolen the sultan's crown?'

'Forgive me,' the man replied. 'I am not here to trouble you. But I must ask you a question or I will not be peaceful even in my grave.'

'Then ask,' Nasruddin said.

'All those years ago,' the man began. 'What was it you were smuggling?'

'That's easy enough,' replied Nasruddin. 'Donkeys.'

About the Author

Shahrukh Husain writes books and films for adults and children. Her children's books include *Demons, Gods and Holy Men from Indian Myth and Legend*, the best-selling *Stories from the Opera*, and six books retelling myths and legends from the ancient civilisations of the world. Her most recent book is *In Search of the Prophet*, stories from the life of Prophet Muhammad.